Goodf...

Tom McLaughlin

*To all my fellow dyslexics
out there – stay strong!*

First published in 2021 in Great Britain by
Barrington Stoke Ltd
18 Walker Street, Edinburgh, EH3 7LP

www.barringtonstoke.co.uk

Text & Illustrations © 2021 Tom McLaughlin

A CIP catalogue record for this book is available
from the British Library upon request

ISBN: 978-1-80090-036-3

Printed by Hussar Books, Poland

CONTENTS

CHAPTER 1

A Pizza the Action

"I can't believe it, Camilla!" said her mum, Deborah, as the Goodfellow family left Camilla's school awards evening. "You won everything there is to win!"

"I know – go me!" Camilla said, grinning as she balanced her awards in her arms.

"Michael, help your sister carry some of her awards, please," Deborah snapped at Camilla's brother. "What if she breaks a nail or something?"

"You're right," Michael said. "I don't know how I'd live with myself."

To the rest of the world the Goodfellows looked like the perfect family. Their mum, Deborah, never had a hair out of place. She was always the first to volunteer whenever there was a bake sale or a school play to be organised. Their dad, Colin, was a dentist. He earned the money that meant they could live in a nice big house and have two new cars.

Camilla was the star of the family. She got straight As at school and divided her time between studying and riding in horse shows. But Michael wasn't so smart. Deborah and Colin were always telling him to be more like his sister. His parents thought he spent too much time watching TV and playing video games. But Michael was sporty, captain of the rugby team. What he lacked in grades he made up for in chasing, catching, throwing and kicking balls.

The Goodfellows were the sort of family who sent Christmas cards with a professional photo of themselves and a long update on how they were doing, despite no one really caring. They were the sort of family who would go to the best restaurant in town and make sure everyone saw them going there. And that's exactly what they were doing right now – going out for dinner to celebrate Camilla's success.

"Colin, grab the door, will you?" Deborah said when they arrived at the restaurant. "A lady should never have to open the door for herself," she added. "I'm famished. Excellent choice of restaurant, Camilla dear. The lobster here is divine. It's the best in town."

"It's the most expensive in town," Colin muttered.

"What did you say, Colin?" Deborah asked. "I think it's only fair to stump up for a good meal after your daughter won every award that she was up for – a first in the history of the school."

Michael sighed. "But some of them aren't even proper awards," he complained. "I mean, is 'best-kept pencil case' really a thing?"

"Well, you'd win awards too, Michael," Deborah said, "if they gave them for jumping around in muddy puddles and watching TV. You are a real, human version of Peppa Pig."

"Rugby is not just jumping in muddy puddles!" Michael argued.

"Shh!" Deborah hissed. "We're going to have a nice time tonight. Your father has been so kind as to book us a table at Cafe Marco, so behave."

"Me, book it?" Colin said as he opened the door to the restaurant. "I thought you had booked the table, dear."

"No, Colin," Deborah said crossly. "I asked *you* to do it several weeks ago."

"Oh dear, I must have forgotten," Colin replied. "But don't worry, dear, I'm sure it will be all right."

"Do you have a reservation, sir?" the waiter asked Colin, twirling his moustache as he spoke.

"Well, this is a tad awkward," Colin said. "No, not exactly – we *nearly* have a reservation. Does that count?"

"What?" the waiter replied. He looked confused.

"I forgot to book a table," Colin explained. "But we come here all the time – well, not all the time; I mean, look at the prices – but we've been here before. Does that help in any way?"

"You'd think it would, but no, sir," the waiter said. "I'm afraid we're fully booked this evening."

"Dad!" Camilla said. "It's my favourite place. You promised we were going to celebrate. This is my night! I want lobster!"

"Maybe they do takeaway!" Michael chuckled.

"I'll throw my medal at you, Michael!" Camilla snapped back.

"You wouldn't dare," said Michael, followed by "Ow!" as Camilla's medal clattered him on the ear.

"Ha!" said Camilla.

"I'll get you for that!" yelled Michael.

"Children, behave! Colin, do something!" screeched Deborah.

"*Stop!*" the waiter yelled. "I will have to ask you to leave. You're upsetting the other customers."

"They seem fine to me!" Deborah said, peering behind the waiter.

"Well, you're upsetting *me* then," the waiter said.

Colin started to panic. "Listen, could we just get a lobster off you?" he asked. "Or we could sit in the bathroom if there's space?"

"The bathroom?" Deborah gasped. "Don't be ridiculous. Colin, slip the waiter some cash," she whispered. "It might help."

"It really won't, *monsieur*," said the waiter.

"I don't have any cash, but I can do contactless," Colin said, and tapped his credit card on the waiter's forehead.

"*Stop it!*" the waiter hissed.

"Congratulations, sis," Michael said to Camilla. "Nothing says well done like eating a cold wet lobster in the toilet!"

"That's it, Michael! You are so *dead*!" Camilla snapped.

"If we could just speak to the owner?" Colin asked.

"I am the owner," the waiter said. "Now, *stop*! You are a horrible family. Please leave my restaurant!"

"What about my dinner?" Camilla asked.

"I'll give you my watch in exchange for a handful of breadsticks!" Colin offered.

"I suggest you go to Gino's," the waiter said. "That seems more your sort of place." He pointed to a restaurant across the road and pushed the Goodfellows out of the door.

"*Gino's!*" Michael yelled, delighted. "Oh, can we? It's brilliant. It's this New York pizza place with a gangster theme."

"Absolutely not," said Deborah.

"Oh, come on. It might be fun," Colin said. "Plus I'm really hungry."

Deborah was also starving. "OK," she said. "But we're coming back here another day!"

"Do Gino's do lobster pizza?" Camilla asked hopefully as they trudged across the road.

"Of course," Michael said.

"Really?" Camilla said, smiling.

"*Noooo!*" Michael laughed. "Ha ha—"

Camilla pinched him.

"Ow! Camilll*llllllla!*" he screeched.

They pushed open the sticky door of Gino's and a waiter greeted them. The place was empty.

"Good evening," the waiter said as he popped gangster hats on all of them. "Welcome to Gino's Pizza. We serve real gangster food, straight up from New York." He was trying to speak in an American accent as he handed them a menu. "My name's Alberto."

"Wait, but you're Nigel, Marjory's son," Deborah said.

"Yeah, I know," Nigel said. "Hello, Mrs Goodfellow. We all have to pretend to be gangsters when we work here. Sometimes I think I'm more of an actor than a waiter!"

"What, you're not really from New York?" Camilla joked.

"I can see I'm going to have great fun serving you tonight, Miss Stuffed Dough Balls," Nigel said.

"What did he call me?" Camilla snapped.

"Can I get anyone some stuffed dough balls?" Nigel asked.

"*Yes!*" Michael said, smiling. "This place is great! Jonny from rugby had a birthday party here. The mud pie was as big as a bike wheel. I mean, it's like being in New York."

The restaurant had been decorated to look like a New York diner, but it wasn't in New York. It was in Tunbridge Wells, a small town in the most English part of England.

Nigel showed the Goodfellows to their seats, then looked at Colin. "What can I get for the godfather?" Nigel asked.

"Ooh, the godfather," Colin replied. "That makes me sound dangerous! I'll take a root beer," Colin said in his best American accent, looking at the menu.

"Don't do the accent," Camilla told her dad, so embarrassed.

"Do you even know what root beer is?" Deborah asked.

"No, not really," Colin said, shrugging. "I just got carried away with it all. Can we have four lemonades and four New Yorker pizzas, please?"

"I'll just have something from the salad bar," Camilla said.

"There ain't no salad bar," Nigel said. "We had a greenfly infestation, so we closed it down. I'll go and put your order in with the chef."

"This place is awful," Deborah said. "The fake accents, the insect problem? It's terrible."

"I love it!" said Michael.

*

"*Pizzas are here! Badaboom badabing!*" Nigel yelled five minutes later, placing them down on the table.

"Already?" Deborah said. "That was fast."

Nigel also put some silver cards on the table.

"What are these?" Michael asked.

"They're scratch cards for a competition to win a trip to the Big Apple," Nigel explained. "That's slang for New York."

"Oh, cool," Michael said. He pulled a slice from his pizza and attacked the scratch card with a 10p coin.

"Where is this meat from?" Camilla asked, pointing at a slice of salami on her pizza.

"Erm, I'm not sure," Nigel said. "I guess the chef can have a look on the packet from the bin if you like? Chef! Where's the meat from?"

"No idea, Alberto," the chef yelled back. "New York? Dunno."

"*New York! Amazing!*" Michael yelled.

"Well, not that amazing," Colin said.

14

"*New York! I can't believe it!*" Michael yelled again.

"Colin, what's wrong with Michael?" Deborah asked. "He seems to be malfunctioning."

"*Look!*" Michael said, holding up the scratch card. "*We won! We are going to New York! Look!*"

Nigel checked the card. "Oh my!" he said. "Crikey, you're right! You won! You really won!"

"We're going to New York?" Camilla said. "I ... I don't know what to do. I have this weird urge to hug you," she said to Michael. He leaned back, looking alarmed.

"We're off to New York?" Deborah said. "Oh my! I need to go shopping – *there's so much shopping to do!*"

"You can do that in New York," Nigel said. "You get spending money as part of the prize. You don't have to pay for a thing – but maybe you could give a tip to the waiter who brought you the scratch card ..."

"I can't believe it," Colin said, grinning. "The Goodfellows are off to America!"

CHAPTER 2

Not So Wise Guys

Meanwhile in a *real* New York restaurant ...

A stocky man with thick eyebrows made a *ching ching* sound with a teaspoon on the side of a wine glass. He stood up to talk to the people in the room.

"Gentlemen, I thank you for your attendance," the man said. "As the boss of the Mancini family, it is a great pleasure to see so many friends and business associates here." He smiled and dabbed the side of his mouth with a napkin.

The man looked round the dimly lit Italian
restaurant. These were no ordinary business
associates – and these weren't ordinary friends.
There is no polite way to say this – they were
gangsters. Mobsters. The sort you see on TV,
from New York, with thick accents and even
thicker necks. These were the sort of people

who would make sure you got whacked if you stepped out of line – and I don't mean round the back of the head with a newspaper. I mean you'd end up swimming with the fishes – chucked in the river to drown, to put it another way. Or you might disappear into a concrete mixer, vanish in a freezer – that kind of thing. Basically you'd end up dead.

This man was Tony Mancini, known as Big T. He was the head of the Mancini gang and a fearsome mobster. Big T's desire for violence and money was matched only by his hunger for spaghetti and meatballs. He was at the restaurant today to talk business.

"It has come to my attention," Big T said, "that a rather large batch of diamonds has arrived in a small store not too far from here. This shipment is very valuable and I am eager to get my hands on it."

There was some nodding and stroking of chins from the gangsters in the room.

"But, as you know, the New York Police Department are making life very difficult for me," Big T went on. "They watch me all the time, thinking that I am up to no good. I find this … very disrespectful."

There was more nodding and mumbling.

"So I have decided to give this work to some business associates from out of town …" Big T said.

A few people in the room started to protest. Big T raised his arms and tried to calm everyone down. "I know, I know, we like to keep things in the family. But there is no way any of us could rob this joint, not with the cops watching us all the time. So four guys from Chicago will do the job for us. They will get their share and we will get ours, and from what I hear there's plenty to go around. We are talking big bucks. It is a small price to pay for a job well done."

"Who are these guys from Chicago?" one gangster asked.

A guy called Jimmy Knuckles replied. He was Big T's most trusted business partner. "They're good," Knuckles said. "I'm picking them up from the airport tomorrow and taking them to the store. They're going to do the job, nice and easy, and they'll deliver the diamonds to Big T's place afterwards. You can meet them then, and we'll have a party to remember. Diamonds and meatballs: am I right or am I right?"

"Ha ha!" Big T laughed, and so did everyone else. "These Chicago guys are the best. Tough guys, mean guys, goodfellas. You know what I mean ... Proper *goodfellas*," Big T said, taking a swig of red wine.

CHAPTER 3

Goodfellows or Goodfellas?

"Goodfellows. *We're the Goodfellows*," Colin said. He waved to the representative from Gino's Pizza – a shiny man there to greet them at the airport in London. The family were ready to set off on their holiday to New York.

"Fantastic! I'm Simon," the representative said. "Congratulations on your win! I have your tickets here. Do you have everything else you need?"

"I think so," Deborah said, checking the passports. "But of course we don't have any

American money – we were told that would be provided as part of the prize."

"Don't worry about that, Mrs Goodfellow," Simon said. "That will be taken care of on your arrival in New York. This trip has a bit of a gangster theme – you know, to match our restaurant. So when you get to New York, a guy called Mr Big will be there to meet you. He'll give you your spending money. Don't be alarmed by how he looks – it's just an actor pretending to be a gangster boss. There will also be a trip to Little Italy and a tour of some of the dangerous parts of New York where some of the most well-known criminals used to live."

"Sounds delightful," Deborah said, smiling nervously.

"Are you ready for your *taste of New York?*" Simon said.

"We are. It's our first time on holiday there," Colin said. "I'd like a cwaaarp of cwaaaarffeeee."

"What?" Simon said, looking confused.

"He's speaking American," Camilla said. "That was 'I'd like a cup of coffee' ... apparently."

They were interrupted by the loudspeaker, which said, "Last call for flight BA 454832 to JFK Airport, boarding now at Gate 4."

"Oh, that's us!" Deborah said. "Come on!"

*

"*New York, whoooooop!*" Michael yelled as they walked off the plane.

"Do you mind?" Camilla said, elbowing him in the ribs. "We are not hooligans – we are

British. I suggest giving the crowds a small wave as we go."

"We're not royalty," Michael said. "We just ate a pizza and got lucky."

"Stop it, you two," Deborah said, putting the family's passports in one of the bags. "Now, let's find Mr Big."

*

Jimmy Knuckles was waiting in the airport Arrivals hall. "Hey, Big T," Knuckles said on his phone, "you got any idea what these guys look like?"

"I dunno," Big T said. "They're keen on disguises. All I know is they will make themselves known to you."

"OK, boss," Knuckles replied. "I'll keep an eye out for some goodfellas."

"Goodfellows ..." Deborah said, overhearing Knuckles. "Yes, that's us! I'm Deborah. This is Colin, my husband, and my children, Camilla and Michael. It's jolly good to meet you."

"You guys?" Knuckles said, looking them up and down.

"Are you the boss, Mr Big?" Michael asked.

"Oh yes, we were told you would have some spending money for us," Colin added.

"Hey, hey!" Knuckles said. "Keep your voice down. The boss sent me to pick you up. He'll give you your money when the job's done. Are you guys ready?"

"I've never been more ready!" Colin smiled.

Knuckles frowned at the four of them again. "Well, I didn't expect you to turn up looking and sounding like British tourists. The disguise is

weird, but if it works, it works! Time for you guys to get a slice of New York!"

"Tally ho!" Deborah said, grinning.

CHAPTER 4

Floor Doughnuts and Diamonds

The streets of New York were busy with traffic.

"I'm driving here!" Knuckles yelled out of his window while honking his horn at the other drivers.

"This isn't the limo I was expecting," Deborah said, looking around the car. "This isn't the driver I was expecting either …"

In the driver's seat, Knuckles lit up a cigar.

Colin smiled nervously. "Well, they did say we would get a taste of America."

"I can taste it all right," Deborah said, coughing as cigar smoke puffed into her face.

"You guys want a doughnut?" Knuckles asked, reaching around on the car floor. "I think I dropped one somewhere up here."

"Yes, please!" Michael said. He was never one to refuse food – even food with car carpet hair stuck on it.

"*No!* I mean, no thank you," Camilla snapped. She dug Michael in the ribs for what felt like the fourteenth time this trip.

The car drove further into the city. For the Goodfellows, it was like being on every film set they'd ever seen – this bit from *Home Alone 2*, that bit from *Spider-Man*. They kept expecting the car to stop, wondering, was it this hotel, was it that one? But Knuckles kept on going until the skyscrapers were nothing but distant shapes in the rear window. Now it still looked like they were driving around a film set, but a scary one – one where you might come to a sticky end.

"It looks a bit grim out there. Where's our hotel?" Deborah asked Colin quietly.

"Maybe this is the gangster tour," Colin said, and shrugged.

"What happened to all the skyscrapers?" Camilla asked.

"You guys really are from out of town. This is the real New York," Knuckles said.

"You see, it's the real America!" Colin said excitedly, taking a picture with his phone. "Anyone can go and see Times Square and the Empire State Building. This is the real bit! Look, there's a man doing a wee in a bin!"

"So, you want your money?" Knuckles said, turning round.

Deborah nodded. "Yes, please."

"Well, this is how you earn it," Knuckles said. "We'll be at the store real soon." He took a puff on his cigar. "The plan is simple – a quick job, in and out."

"What's he talking about?" Deborah whispered to Colin.

"I've no idea," Colin said.

"The place is called Hersh's Diamond Store," Knuckles said. "They've got a shipment of diamonds that has just arrived – real beauties too. You've just got to go in and steal them. Don't kill anyone unless you have to. Here, take this." Knuckles handed them a bag. "Use what you gotta use, do what you gotta do. Two minutes, in and out."

Colin looked in the bag. It was filled with guns: big ones, small ones, medium ones. They were cold, heavy and dangerous looking. "Right ..."

Suddenly Knuckles' phone started to ring. "I gotta take this," he said. "Yo, Stevo, what are we doing with the guy who won't pay up?"

"That bag is full of guns," Camilla said.

"I know!" Colin whispered so that Knuckles wouldn't hear. "Perhaps it's like one of those pretend adventure holidays, you know? We have to show our loyalty to Mr Big and carry out an armed robbery to earn our spending money … maybe? Like a game show – a really grim game show."

"It doesn't feel like this is pretending," Deborah said, holding up one of the guns. "Did Knuckles say he was actually from Gino's Pizza? He's not shiny and happy like Simon, is he?"

"Well, now you mention it, not really," Colin mumbled.

"So he could be a real actual gangster?" Camilla said. "But how did he know our names?"

"Well, goodfella in American means gangster," Michael said. "I saw it in a film."

They stopped talking as Knuckles ended his phone call.

"I don't know!" Knuckles said, hanging up. "It's almost like people *want* you to break their bones. Why don't they just pay up?"

"Tell me, do you like Gino's Pizza?" Deborah asked Knuckles.

"Never heard of it," he replied. "Is that the place on the corner of 49th Street that got closed down because of a rat thing? Listen, there'll be plenty of time to grab a bite after the job." Knuckles pulled the car up to a slow stop. "We're here now. Remember, in and out, as little death and destruction as possible. Big T doesn't want any trouble with the cops. That's why we got you guys in. We want a nice clean job – got it?"

Everyone nodded. They didn't want to argue with a man like Knuckles, who puffed on cigars and ate floor doughnuts.

"Now go!" he barked.

The Goodfellows got out of the car nervously. They looked over the road. There was Hersh's Diamond Store. It was a busy, bustling day in New York. The wind was cold and biting. The Goodfellows realised that there was nothing pretend about this – it wasn't a stop on a sightseeing tour. This was really happening. Knuckles was a real gangster and that was a real diamond store that they were meant to rob.

"What do we do?" Camilla asked.

"I've got a plan. We could run away?" Colin said.

"Run away? Are you mad?" Michael said. "To where? We don't know where we're going and we don't even have our bags. They're in the boot of the car."

"Oh ..." Colin said.

"Come on, Colin. That was a useless plan!" Deborah scolded him.

"Look, I'm a dentist from Kent," Colin said. "I'm not an expert at escaping from robbers."

"This isn't just a robber – these guys are the mafia!" Michael said. "The real deal! Knuckles mentioned a guy called Big T. He's the number one gangster in New York. You don't want to mess with him."

"How do you know so much about this?" Deborah asked.

"Yeah?" Camilla added.

"I watched a documentary about it, and I've seen loads of gangster films," Michael said. "I know all about this stuff."

"I thought when you weren't at rugby, you were busy with your homework, not watching TV," Deborah said, looking annoyed. "We will talk about this later."

"Well, I could have been studying algebra, but at this moment, I'm glad I didn't," Michael snapped. "The stuff I've learned from watching TV is going to be far more useful!"

"All right, Mr Expert, what would you do?" Deborah asked Michael. She looked back at Knuckles, who was watching them from the car.

"Well, we go into the diamond shop before Knuckles gets suspicious," Michael said. "Then, once we're in, we tell the owner what's going on. He can call the police and we get out of this whole mess." Michael shrugged. "That's what I would do."

"That's actually a pretty good plan," Colin admitted. "OK, family vote. All in favour, nod."

Everyone nodded.

"That's agreed then," Colin said. "Welcome to America – off we go to pretend to rob the diamond shop."

CHAPTER 5

This Is Not a Robbery

"What can I do for you?" a man said as the Goodfellows all entered the diamond store. They guessed this was Hersh.

Colin was carrying the large bag of guns. The place was brightly lit, which made the hundreds of diamonds on the shelves dazzle. Camilla's jaw dropped.

"This isn't a robbery, so please don't think that it is," Colin said with what he hoped was a reassuring smile.

"Did you say robbery?" Hersh said, panicking.

"Yes!" Colin said. "But don't worry, this isn't one. We're hoping you can help us, you see. There's a dangerous gangster sitting in a car outside and he's sent us in here to carry out a robbery."

"What's in the bag?" Hersh asked.

"Some guns," Colin said apologetically. He lifted a gun out of the bag and held it up to show Hersh. "But we don't want to use them."

Hersh put his hands up. He looked terrified.

"You probably want to call the police," Deborah said.

"Don't worry, I won't!" Hersh said, shaking his head.

"No, you should call them!" Camilla said.

"Look, just take what you want!" Hersh
yelled.

"It's fine, no one's going to get hurt," Colin said. He placed the bag of guns down.

"Please don't hurt me," Hersh said. "I'll give you the jewels – what are you after? I've got loads. Here, take the lot. I'll put them in a bag for you."

"But what about the police?" Camilla said.

"Don't worry about that," Hersh said. "I won't get the police involved."

*

Thirty seconds later, the Goodfellows left Hersh's Diamond Store with a huge bag full of jewels.

"Well, good work, everyone," Colin said. "Our first attempt at not robbing a place ended with us robbing the place. Bravo. Bravo indeed."

"Not being a robber is much harder than it looks," Michael said, and shrugged.

"Well, it was a silly plan," Camilla snapped.

"There was nothing wrong with the plan!"
Michael insisted.

"So what now?" Deborah asked.

"Maybe if we give Knuckles the stuff,
he'll drop us back at the airport," Colin said

hopefully. "Then we can go home, back to Kent, and pretend this never happened."

"Whoa!" Knuckles said. He took the bag and looked at the stash of diamonds. "I heard you guys were good, but look at all this loot. This is even more than Big T asked for."

"What can I say?" Deborah said, smiling. "If a job's worth doing, it's worth doing well ... That's what my mum always used to say – even if it was mainly about baking scones and not armed robbery."

Knuckles smiled. "It's time to go see Big T and get your money. But this is so good, I reckon he might have a few other jobs for you. Come on, let's go."

It was clear the Goodfellows wouldn't be going back home to Kent yet.

"Well, we'd be mad to turn down a meeting with Big T ..." Colin sighed.

The Goodfellows got back into the car for another journey across New York.

After a while, the streets changed from shops and tower blocks to leafy suburbs. The houses got grander as the city disappeared behind them. Some houses had tennis courts and swimming pools – two swimming pools, even!

The car slowed down outside one of the houses and turned into a long drive. The house was huge, maybe even the size of a leisure centre. It was surrounded by big walls and spiky fences, and there were security guards and cameras everywhere.

"We're here," Knuckles said gruffly. "Let's go see the big man."

The Goodfellows got out of the car and looked at the gigantic house. "Everything is so much bigger in America," Camilla said.

"You're telling me. Look at the size of him," Colin said, pointing.

A man in a vest was opening the front door. He was the size of a wardrobe – a large wardrobe. He was sucking on a cigar. His hairy body could hardly fit inside his vest and his large head popped out over the top, making it look like he had no neck.

"I wouldn't want to get on the wrong side of him," Deborah said.

"He might eat you," Michael added.

"Shh!" Colin said.

"There he is. Big T ... the boss," Knuckles said, leading the way.

Knuckles and Big T kissed each other on the cheeks, and Knuckles whispered something to him before the Goodfellows reached the door.

"Knuckles says you guys did good," Big T said, looking in the bag. "Quite a haul. He said you had these crazy British accents too. Nice, a good touch. I told everyone you guys were the best. How's Crazy Eddie? Still the King of Chicago?"

"Errrr ... yep!" Deborah said, smiling. "He's ... er ... mad as a bag of badgers."

"Well, OK," Big T said, looking confused. He ushered them into the house. "Come on in, guys. There's a few associates of mine I'd like you to meet."

The Goodfellows followed Big T inside nervously.

The house was full of odd people. They were dressed like they were in a film: thick dark glasses, hats, chunky jewellery, and they were sipping tiny drinks with ice in them and eating salami. There was lots of smoking and nodding.

There must have been thirty or forty people inside.

"Here's my cousin Pauley," Big T said, introducing the Goodfellows to people as they walked past. "And this is Little Vinny. He's from the Upper East Side."

"Hi, Little Vinny!" Michael said with a smile.

"Why are you still doing that stooopid British voice?" Big T asked, looking at Michael sternly. "You're among friends now. You can drop the disguises." He handed them a briefcase. "I got something for you! This is your cash. Why don't you go and freshen up, and then we can talk about another job. There's this bank, you see, and I would like to make a withdrawal, if you know what I mean." Big T chuckled and showed the Goodfellows down the corridor towards one of the rooms.

"Oh," Colin said, smiling and taking the briefcase. "Thanks!"

The family headed down the corridor, their pace getting faster until they were practically running. They reached the doorway Big T had pointed out and rushed in, quickly closing the door behind them.

"What are we going to do?" Camilla asked.

49

"I don't know," Deborah said.

"We need a plan," Michael said.

"Any ideas, Colin?" Deborah snapped.

"*Dad?*" Camilla yelled when Colin didn't answer.

Colin had opened the briefcase and was speechless for a moment.

He showed it to the others. "Look at this," Colin said. "Look at all this money. There's got to be thousands here, hundreds of thousands. What are we going to do? We have a briefcase of cash and a bag of stolen diamonds with our fingerprints on them."

"That's not the worst of it," Michael said.

CHAPTER 6

The Great Escape

"What do you mean, 'That's not the worst of it'?" Deborah asked Michael.

"We're on TV," Michael said, pointing at the screen in the room.

"Eh?" Deborah said. She grabbed the remote and turned the volume up so they could hear the news presenter.

"There was a jewellery robbery today in Hersh's Diamond Store," the presenter said. "Four people – two male, two female – stole almost six million dollars' worth of diamonds and other precious jewels. Police are on the lookout for these people, believed to be British. They are considered dangerous."

Images from security cameras popped up on the TV, showing the Goodfellows' grainy black and white faces. "The police believe that the robbery may be linked to mafia crime boss Tony Mancini, but at the moment they have no evidence."

Then a familiar picture flashed up on the TV – it was the man who'd greeted them a few moments ago, Big T. "Tony Mancini is considered one of New York's most dangerous gangsters. He is suspected of the murders of over a dozen people, but the police have never been able to pin anything on him ..."

Michael turned round to see his dad closing up the briefcase and moving towards the door. "What are you doing?" he asked.

"Well, I was going to give this back to Big T, explain what has happened and go and find our hotel," Colin said.

"I don't think it's as simple as that, Dad!" Camilla said, shaking her head. "Plus Big T's entire gang is out there waiting for us."

"Colin, listen to your daughter," Deborah said.

Bang, bang! There was a loud knock at the door. "Come on out and get a drink," Knuckles said.

"*Yes*, we'll be right there!" Colin yelled, adding, "What are we going to do? The window! We can escape!" Colin ran over, but unsurprisingly the window was locked.

"We need to return the diamonds to Hersh's shop and tell the police everything," Deborah said. She looked out of the window at the guards, dogs and rather large walls. "But it seems Big T has an awful lot of security ..."

"Look past the trees. That's Knuckles' car!" Colin said, pointing. "If we sneak outside, I reckon we could get it going and use it to escape!"

"But how do we get out there?" Camilla asked.

"Just go back the way we came," Colin said. "Through the front door, grabbing the diamonds as we go ...?" His voice trailed off as he heard the idea coming out of his mouth.

"Steal from the big murdering bad man?" Camilla asked.

"Errr ... yep," Colin agreed.

"I'm not sure that's going to work, Dad!" Camilla sighed, fed up.

"We need to pretend," Michael said. "Pretend to be gangsters. I've watched enough TV to know how these things go."

"What do you mean?" Camilla asked.

"Look, we don't have another choice," Michael said. "Big T's gang are bound to be suspicious of us if we keep talking in our British accents. But if we pretend to be gangsters, we can blend into the crowd. They'll stop paying so much attention to us. Then, when Big T isn't watching, we pick up the diamonds and sneak outside. Remember, when we didn't know we were gangsters, everyone treated us like gangsters. We just have to believe it. Fake it till you make it, baby." Michael smiled.

"OK, OK," Deborah said. "You have exactly two minutes to teach us how to be gangsters. We can do it. If I can put on the school nativity without a Joseph at the last minute because he had tummy trouble, we can do this! We have to do this ..."

CHAPTER 7

Golf Drive

"Right, everyone," Michael said, taking charge. "I've got some great ideas about how to behave like a gangster, from TV shows and all the video games I've played."

"Do you ever do any schoolwork?" Colin muttered.

"Not the time, Dad," Michael sighed.

"OK, carry on," Colin muttered back.

"You will have seen that real-life gangsters do not say much," Michael said. "They nod, and they only say things like 'hey' and 'sure'. This is good. The less we say, the better. Shrug when you're asked a question." Michael shrugged. The others copied him. "Hold your hands out and frown. When it comes to talking, if we have to use words, say them in an American accent. After me: 'Hey, Big T'."

Everyone took a turn saying it.

"Bravo, Mum. You're a natural," Michael said. "Well done, Camilla. Now, Dad, excellent enthusiasm, but you sound … well, Welsh. Try again. It might help to channel the voice of an American movie star, like you're doing an impression."

"I can only do one American impression," Colin said.

"Who?" Michael asked.

"Homer Simpson? Hey, Bart!" Colin said, shrugging and frowning all at the same time. "I mean, Big T."

"Well, that will have to do!" Michael said. "Now I want everyone to imagine they've got a cold, a real stinker. It'll give you a proper New York accent."

"Hey, Big D," everyone repeated as if they had a blocked nose.

"Whaaachooooo!" Colin added at the end of his turn.

"Not *that* coldy," Michael said. "Right, stay in character, guys. We are badass gangsters from Chicago. Now, remember the plan. We go out there and blend into the crowd. Don't do anything to draw attention to yourselves. And when nobody is looking, we go out of the front door as fast as we can. I'll grab the diamonds."

"And once we're outside, we run to Knuckles' car," Colin said. "Michael, imagine that bag of diamonds is a rugby ball and you need to score the winning try. Let's go."

"And remember, American accents," Camilla said. "We have to stay in character!"

They all walked out of the door, shrugging and muttering "hey" under their breaths. They got back to the room where the gangsters were waiting and Colin helped himself to a drink. "D'oh!" he said.

"Hey … ho … hey," Michael said, grabbing some salami.

"Have you got any tea, T?" Deborah said. "I am dotally parched."

"Uh-oh," Camilla said under her breath. "We're toast."

"You guys are acting pretty strange," Big T said. "Those accents. I mean, what's going on? Which part of Chicago are you from?"

"Lower ... downtown ..." Colin said.

"Yeah, on the east side, between 54th Street and 3292nd," Michael said.

"I was born in Chicago," another gangster said. "There ain't no 3292nd Street!"

Suddenly all the gangsters were staring at the Goodfellows.

"I think we should probably leave!" Colin whispered. "*Ruuun!*"

Michael ran as fast as he could. He grabbed the bag of diamonds from the table and swerved round a couple of bad guys. He spotted Camilla standing near the door.

"Siiiiiiis," Michael yelled, and threw the perfect pass to her. Camilla grabbed the bag mid-air and ran out of the door.

"Nice catch!" Michael shouted after her.

The Mancini gang may have been many things: dangerous, terrifying, murderers. But one thing they weren't was fit – all those meatball sandwiches had taken their toll. The Goodfellows easily outran them in the 50-metre dash down the drive to Knuckles' car.

"Ah ..." Colin grabbed the car door handle and stopped.

"What?" Deborah said, looking backwards.

"It's locked!" Colin shrugged.

"Look, I don't want to alarm anyone, but the people chasing us have guns," Camilla yelled.

"Break the window!" Michael said.

"*No*, it'll really hurt!" Colin yelled. Then he spotted something. "Never mind, we're changing to *Plan B*! We're taking that!" Colin pointed to another vehicle that was parked on the drive. But this was no ordinary set of wheels.

"It's a … golf cart!" Camilla screamed. "It doesn't even have doors!"

But they didn't really have much choice.

"*Just get in!*" Deborah cried.

Peeeeeooooow! A bullet went whistling past their ears.

"They're shooting at us! Colin, drive!" Deborah said, looking back. Big T and his gang of hoodlums were all piling into Jimmy Knuckles' car. "*Go!*"

CHAPTER 8

Round the Bend

"Get over to the other side of the road, Colin!" Deborah screamed as a bus headed straight towards them.

The Goodfellows were racing back through the city towards Hersh's Diamond Store. They hoped to put an end to this mess once and for all by returning the diamonds to Hersh and telling the police how they happened to commit armed robbery within forty minutes of arriving in America.

"Ooops, sorry! Mirror, signal, manoeuvre," Colin said. He stuck his arm out like a cyclist and moved over to the right-hand side of the road.

"I'm not sure this is a good plan," Camilla said, looking behind her. "I don't know if we can outrun Big T in this thing."

"Especially with Dad driving," Michael added.

"Oi! I've got over twenty years of no-claims bonuses under my belt!" Colin yelled.

"No offence, dear, but you do drive like a vicar," Deborah agreed.

"I thought I was pretty good behind the wheel," Colin said, getting annoyed.

"You're safe. Safe is good – normally!" Camilla said, looking back. "But they're gaining on us. What we need now isn't safe, but fast."

"I'll take it from here, Dad," Michael said, putting on his sunglasses.

"What?" Colin yelled.

"Don't worry, Dad. All these years of playing *Grand Drift 7: Road to Hell* are about to pay off."

"I don't know what those words mean," Colin shouted.

"It's a driving game, Dad," Michael explained. "One you play on a computer."

"But you're too young to drive," Colin yelled.

"To be honest, Dad, our list of crimes already includes armed robbery, handling stolen cash and associating with known criminals," Michael said. "I think driving without a licence is pretty small compared to all that."

"He's right. And he's really good at driving games!" Camilla added.

"Thanks, sis. Now, don't move yet," Michael yelled to Colin. He sat on Colin's lap and took the wheel. "Now move your foot off the pedal and slide out of the driver's seat." Colin carefully slid away, leaving Michael to drive the golf cart.

"Right, let's see what this baby can do," Michael said. "Hang on, everyone." He pushed his foot down on the pedal and skidded into a side alley.

*

Meanwhile in Knuckles' car ...

"Hey, where did they go?" Big T said. "You lost them, Knuckles!" He looked out of the car window. "Who are these guys? Because they sure ain't wise guys from Chicago."

"Well, they found me at the airport," Knuckles replied. "They said, 'We're the

Goodfellows,' in those British accents. They looked just like tourists. I thought it was a good disguise … but I guess it wasn't a disguise after all."

"Goodfell*ows*?" said Big T. "Not goodfell*as*! So what you are saying is that they're just a bunch of tourists who are called Goodfellows? Oh, this is a mess – everything we've said to them, everything they've seen – they could bring us all down!" Big T clipped the back of Knuckles' head. *"And they got my diamonds too! We need to catch them!"*

"I'm sorry, boss, but the kid clearly knows how to drive a car," Knuckles said. "I'm finding it hard to keep up."

"It's not a car – it's a golf cart! And it only does twenty miles an hour! Go faster!"

"Sorry, boss. But we're … carrying a lot of extra weight," Knuckles said, looking in the rear mirror at the seven gangsters in the back.

"What do you mean by that?" Big T snapped. "Are you calling Big Vinny, Big Sam, Big McDuff, Big Jim, Big Sal, Big Pauley and Big Sonny fat or something?"

"No, boss," Knuckles said. "I just meant the guns and stuff, you know."

CHAPTER 9

A Stinker of a Day

Back in the golf cart ...

"Well, I have some bad news!" Colin yelled. "And good news."

"What?" Camilla asked.

"Well, the good news is that we're very close," Colin said, checking the sat-nav on his phone. "Next right, Michael!"

Michael swerved around the corner.

"And the bad news?" Deborah said.

"It seems someone else is following us," Colin said, looking up.

"Oh good, a helicopter – and a police one at that!" Deborah sighed. "This is turning into a real stinker of a day."

"I wonder how the police found us?" Michael asked.

"I know," Camilla said. "It's a mystery how the police could have seen something as innocent-looking as a car full of gangsters chasing a golf cart around New York. This is *the most* ridiculous car chase in the history of car chases. In fact, I'm not even sure you can count it as a car chase as there's only one car involved!"

"I am doing my best! Anyway, I have more bad news," Michael said, looking at the red flashing light inside the golf cart. "We're almost out of battery."

"Are you kidding?" Camilla cried out.

"*No!*"

"How much further is it to the diamond shop?" Camilla asked.

"It's along this street. We just keep going straight," Colin said.

"I've got an idea!" Camilla said. She'd noticed some rope in the back of the golf cart. "We practise this at pony club, in case a horse runs away. You see that bin lorry up ahead? I'll make a loop at the end of the rope and throw it. If I can hook it onto the lorry, we can hitch a ride all the way up the street to the diamond shop."

Camilla started swinging the rope around her head and then threw it towards the back of the lorry.

"Got it! Hold on!" Camilla yelled. The cart began to speed up as the lorry pulled them towards the diamond store.

*

In Knuckles' car...

"What are they doing, Knuckles?" Big T asked as the gangsters' car got closer to the golf cart.

"I dunno, boss," Knuckles said. "These guys are either idiots or geniuses. They appear to be trying to catch a garbage truck like it's a runaway cow."

"I'm sick of these guys," Big T growled. "Mow them down, all of them, or shoot them off the road. I want this over with."

"We got company in the sky, boss," Big Sal said, spotting the police helicopter. "We better not do anything they could arrest us for."

"*I hate this day!*" Big T said.

Big Vinny craned his neck to look out of the window at the Goodfellows. "Where are they going?"

"Oh no. I think I know," Knuckles said.

"Where?" Big T asked.

"They're going back to the scene of the crime: the diamond store," Knuckles said, recognising the area. "Shall we scarper, boss?"

"No," said Big T. "I want to make them pay for what they did to us – hustling us and making us look like fools."

"Right, boss," Big Sam said. "Because we don't need anyone to make us look like fools – we can do that all by ourselves. Is that what you mean?"

"Yeah ..." All the other gangsters nodded too.

"Oh, give me strength," Big T muttered.

*

In the golf cart ...

"We're losing them!" Colin said. Behind them, Big T's car had got caught in traffic.

"*Look!* There's the diamond shop," Camilla yelled. "Mum, pass me your nail scissors."

Camilla used the scissors to cut the golf cart free of the bin lorry, just as Michael pulled them to a stop outside the store.

"This is going to take some explaining," Colin said, looking nervous. He turned to Deborah. "Darling, you better do it."

"Me?" she said, horrified.

"Look," said Colin. "I've seen you return a pair of pyjamas with a scuff mark on them to M&S with no proof of purchase and without the label on. Yet within five minutes, you had a new pair and the shop manager had given you a gift voucher and a bunch of flowers as an apology. You are the greatest negotiator there has ever been. The UN should have made you secretary-general. You're up!" Colin passed Deborah the bag of diamonds. "No offence, but complaining and arguing about stuff is what you do best. It's why I married you."

"Well, I suppose you're right that I am very skilled at dealing with salespeople," Deborah said, taking a deep breath. "Right, here we go!"

CHAPTER 10

A Crazy Confession

At the door of Hersh's Diamond Store, some police officers were busy taking notes and dusting for prints.

"Hello!" Deborah said cheerfully, barging her way past them. "I'd like to see the manager, please. I wish to make a complaint!"

Inside the store, Hersh was talking to another officer.

"That's her, Detective Harrison! That's ... all of them," Hersh said, looking amazed as he pointed to the Goodfellows. "You can't rob me again, you took everything!"

"What the—?" Detective Harrison said, and spun round.

"Ah, you're the man I want to see," Deborah said. She slammed down the bag of jewels on the counter.

"What's going on here?" Detective Harrison said, pulling out his badge. "Police! Hands where I can see them."

"Yes, well, I'm very angry," Deborah snapped. "I came in here earlier with the express desire not to rob the place. Yet, despite my best efforts, this man let us rob the place. It's shocking, really, when you think about it."

"What?" Hersh said.

"Eh?" Detective Harrison said.

"You see, it all started back in England," Deborah went on. "You know England? It used to run this country before, well, America became America ... Anyway, we won a competition in a pizza restaurant. A restaurant with a gangster theme."

"A restaurant that has a criminal theme?" Detective Harrison said.

"I know, it's just plain wrong, right?" Deborah said. "Because there is nothing funny about crime. Anyway, we won a trip to New York, your lovely city here. When we arrived at the airport, we were picked up by a man who calls himself Knuckles." Deborah leaned in. "Between you and me, I don't think that's his real name. Anyway, he thought we were some goodfellas, which I believe is a word for gangsters. We're the Goodfellows, but he thought we were goodfellas. Knuckles thought our accents were part of a disguise. And we thought this was a big joke, like a themed holiday – live life in New York like a gangster. So, before we knew it, Mr Knuckles had brought us here to rob Hersh's Diamond Store. He gave us a load of guns and told us to get all these diamonds for Big T."

"This Knuckles guy is part of Big T's crew?" Detective Harrison asked.

"So it would seem," Deborah said. "We quickly realised it wasn't a themed holiday at all. So we came in here hoping that Hersh would call the police and help us out. We told him we weren't robbing him, but he still made us rob him. Now, I'm not suggesting you charge Hersh with a crime. He was probably in shock. But you can check the security tapes. We did not rob him. He handed everything over to us."

"I got the tape right here, Detective," another officer said, hitting play. They all leaned over and watched the security tape. It was a bit fuzzy, but you could make out who it was and what they were saying.

"What can I do for you?"

"This isn't a robbery, so please don't think that it is."

"Did you say robbery?"

"Yes! But don't worry, this isn't one. We're hoping you can help us, you see. There's a dangerous gangster sitting in a car outside and he's sent us in here to carry out a robbery."

"What's in the bag?"

"Some guns. But we don't want to use them."

"You probably want to call the police."

"Don't worry, I won't!"

"No, you should call them!"

"Look, just take what you want!"

"Well, I'll be ..." Detective Harrison said. "They're telling the truth ..."

"You believe their story?" Hersh said, looking stunned.

"It's so ridiculous that it has to be true. No normal person could ever come up with such a crazy lie."

"Thank you." Colin smiled. "I think."

"So I would like to apologise, on behalf of the Goodfellows," Deborah said, "for robbing the diamond shop despite our best efforts not to. Here is everything that we took, all returned. You can count it."

"Errr ... thank you," Hersh said, grabbing the bag.

"I don't suppose there's a reward for finding all the jewels and returning them, is there?" Camilla said, eyeing a big ruby.

"No, there isn't," Hersh said, clutching his stolen property closer.

"I gotta get something straight," Detective Harrison said. "You said Big T was involved. We've been trying to put him away for years."

"Oh yes, he is," Deborah confirmed.

"Can you prove that?" Detective Harrison asked.

"Well, why don't you ask him yourself?" Deborah said, pointing as Knuckles drove his car towards the front of the store.

"He is going to brake, isn't he?" Michael yelled.

Smaaash!

CHAPTER 11

The End for Big T

Everyone fell to the ground as glass shattered everywhere. Knuckles had driven the car right into the store.

"When I said get me as close to the store as possible, I didn't mean ..." Big T yelled. "Oh, never mind." He pulled out a gun. "Where are my diamonds?"

"Nobody move! Police!" Detective Harrison screamed as he and his officers pulled out their guns.

"I want my diamonds. They got stolen!" Big T yelled, pointing at Deborah and Colin.

"You're complaining that the diamonds were stolen?" Hersh yelled. "You stole them from me!"

"No I didn't – *they* did!" Big T said, pointing at the Goodfellows.

"*He* told us to!" Deborah said, pointing at Knuckles.

"Well, *he* told me to tell them to!" Knuckles said, pointing at Big T.

"Thank you. That proves the conspiracy to commit a crime," Detective Harrison said. "There's a long prison sentence coming your way, Big T. Now put your gun down!"

"I'm thinking maybe it wasn't such a good idea to follow these guys after all, boss ..." Knuckles whispered. "We're a bit outnumbered."

Big T looked around him and realised that it was over. "Fine, I'll confess everything, Officer," he sighed. "But can you promise me one thing? I don't want to end up in prison with these goons." He nodded to the other gangsters. "Lock me up anywhere, just away from these idiots."

"But, boss …" Knuckles complained.

"Cuff the lot of them and take them away!" Detective Harrison said.

"What about these guys?" one of the officers asked, pointing at the Goodfellows.

"Let them go."

"Thank you, Detective," Deborah said, smiling.

"You're welcome," Detective Harrison replied. "You must be rewarded for helping us put away one of the most infamous gangs in the country.

I'd like to offer you a stay at one of the grandest hotels in the city and a slap-up dinner at a top restaurant."

"You can do that?" Deborah gasped.

"I sure can!" Detective Harrison said, smiling. "Just do me a favour and don't go to any more diamond stores while you're here."

"Deal!" Colin said.

"There is one question I have," Detective Harrison added. "What happened to the original goodfellas who flew in from Chicago?"

*

In a different part of town ...

Four goodfellas had just finished watching a theatre show.

"Johnny, when do you think this diamond robbery is going to begin?" one of the goodfellas asked. "I mean, going to a Broadway musical is great fun, but what about some real gangster work? Are you crying, Johnny?"

"No ... well, you are too," Johnny said. "I'm sorry, it's just been such an emotional day."

"I know, boss. It's really been something.
We turn up at the airport to do a job, but then
Mr Big gives us all that money, a fancy lunch
in a restaurant – and that gangster tour of
New York. And then tickets to *The Lion King* on
Broadway. I'm gonna be humming the 'Circle
of Life' all night now. Pass me the hankie …
whoooowhooooo."

"I think I'm gonna call my dad," another
goodfella said. "It's about time we reconnected,
before it's too late. I don't want to end up like
Simba. Boss, maybe we should think about a
change of career?"

"Like what?" Johnny said, dabbing his eyes.

"Well, we always talked about opening a
little tea shop by the coast. I bet you're not
likely to get murdered if you work with fondant
fancies."

"Let's do it!" Johnny said, hugging his pal.

CHAPTER 12

We Are the Goodfellows

The next day, the Goodfellow family were cruising down the streets of Manhattan in a limo.

"Well, this is a treat. Look at this," Colin said. He held up a newspaper with a photo of the Goodfellows on the front page. "We're heroes and superstars! We've got a lot to put in the Goodfellow family newsletter this year!"

Michael smiled. "And all thanks to computer games and watching TV!"

"Yes, who knew!" Deborah said. "I never thought I'd hear myself say this, but I want you to spend more time in front of a screen, Michael."

"Yes, well done, little brother," Camilla said, leaning in. "When we get back, you can have the medal I got at school for being all-round best person ever."

"Are you going to hug me?" Michael asked, surprised.

"Maybe, yes, I thought about it. Why?" Camilla snapped.

"Nothing. That would be nice," Michael said, hugging her back.

"No time for that now. We're here!" Deborah said as the limo pulled up outside a grand restaurant.

A snooty-looking waiter was waiting at the restaurant door.

"Can I help you?" the waiter asked.

"Table for the Goodfellows," Deborah said, smiling politely.

"I'm sorry, we have a no-sneakers policy," the waiter said, looking at Michael's shoes. "Perhaps the place over the road would be more suitable?"

Everyone turned around to see a pizza bar.

"Sneakers? You mean trainers?" Deborah said. "You're not letting us in because of that?" She shook her head.

"Leave this to me, dear," Colin said, and turned to the waiter. "I'm not sure you understood what my wife said. It wasn't a request or a suggestion, it was a fact. We have a table booked and we are coming in, and we

will order what we want. We have been shot
at, chased, accused of robbery, and we helped
to catch this city's most feared gangsters. So
you are letting us in, whether we're wearing
sneakers, roller skates or turnips on our heads.
We are the Goodfellows and we will not be
messed around any more!"

More
HILARIOUS FUN
as the Royal Family
have to rough it!

Tom McLaughlin

Queen
of King Street

ISBN: 978-1-78112-939-5